I'll Be There

For my mom
A. S.

For Rebecca and Nora
M. P.

I'll Be There

Ann Stott

illustrated by Matt Phelan

CANDLEWICK PRESS

Did you push me in a carriage
when I was a baby?

Yes, I took you to the playground . . .

and pushed you way up high on the swing.

I dressed you in stripes

and fed you squished peas.

I gave you bubble baths in the
kitchen sink

and wrapped you in your favorite
blanket to keep you warm.

When you got tired, I carried you up to bed

and read your favorite bedtime story.

When you were a baby, I did lots of things for you.

Now you can do them on your own.

I know. I can tie my own shoes

and pick out my own clothes.

I take showers now

and sometimes go to sleep after you!

I can read my own bedtime story

and even make breakfast for you!

Yes, you are growing up.

Will you still take care of me
when I'm big?

Well, you can tie your own shoes and read your own bedtime story.

But I am your mom, and that will never change.

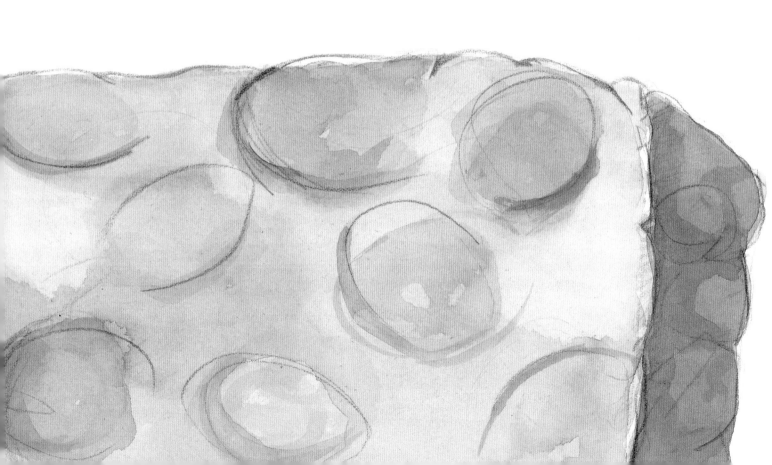

Even when you're big, I'll be there.